STARRING
Jules

(SUPER-SECRET SPY GIRL)

BETH AIN

Illustrated by Anne Keenan Higgins

Scholastic Inc.
★ ★ ★

No part of this publication may be reproduced, stored in a retrieval system, or transmitted in any form or by any means, electronic, mechanical, photocopying, recording, or otherwise, without written permission of the publisher. For information regarding permission, write to Scholastic Inc., Attention: Permissions Department, 557 Broadway, New York, NY 10012.

This book was originally published in hardcover by Scholastic Press in 2014.

ISBN 978-0-545-44357-9

Text copyright © 2014 by Beth Ain
Illustrations copyright © 2014 by Scholastic Inc.
All rights reserved. Published by Scholastic Inc.
SCHOLASTIC and associated logos are trademarks
and/or registered trademarks of Scholastic Inc.

Designed by Natalie C. Sousa

12 11 10 9 8 7 6 5 4 3 2 1   15 16 17 18 19 20/0

Printed in the U.S.A.   40
This edition first printing, March 2015

for
JON
(my all-time favorite
road-trip companion)

Lights! Camera! Action!

Read along as Jules Bloom's star
continues to rise:

Starring Jules (as herself)
Starring Jules (in drama-rama)
Starring Jules (super-secret spy girl)
Starring Jules (third grade debut)

CONTENTS

last lists, old-timey songs, and the last-day-of-school blues

"Earth to Julesium!" Teddy says, knocking into me hard.

"Teddy!" I say. "It's the last day. You couldn't even *not* knock into me on the last day of school?" I always say that Teddy feels like a Super Ball bouncing all around the room, but lately it feels like he's got special superglue on him that only seems to stick to me.

"Well, you were just standing there, staring at your cubby," he says.

"Well, maybe I like just standing there, staring at my cubby. Ever think of that?" I say. I find my seat and look around the classroom. The blankety-blank blankness of what used to be the perfect second-grade classroom. FAMOUS WOMEN OF MATHEMATICS poster? Gone. Perfectly perfect cursive handwriting charts? Gone. Dirty, not-even-a-little-bit-white walls? Here to stay. Second grade is over.

"Hiya, Jules," Elinor says.

"Don't bother," I hear Teddy say to her. "She just wants to stare at things. She hates the last day of school."

"Really?" Elinor asks. "Who hates the last day of school?"

I see Charlotte listening to everyone talking about me like I'm not there and I can just tell she's going to have something to say about it.

"Jules Bloom, that's who," she says.

Elinor clears her throat and squats down next to my desk. "But it's summer, Jules. 'No more teachers, no more books . . .'" She looks around. "Do you sing that song in this country?"

Charlotte shakes her head no and gives a terrible Charlotte snort at the thought.

"Yes," I say, coming to Elinor's rescue, "my parents do, but they're kind of old."

"It's summer, Jules!" Elinor says now, standing up. "And you're going to film a real, live movie with megastar Rick Hinkley and teen star Emma Saxony, and I'm going to London to see my dad, and we're going to be pen pals, and Teddy will be at science camp, and Charlotte's going to sleepaway."

"Well, that part's pretty good, I guess." I look at Charlotte and smile a fake smile.

"Not just any sleepaway, you know," Charlotte says. "Camp Lackahanna." She puts up big jazz hands when she says this.

"It's a camp for performing arts. Celebrity kids go there."

"Wow," I say.

"Emma Saxony went there." Charlotte is obsessed with Emma Saxony. "And they have golf carts we get to ride around in, and campfires, and zip lines, and trampolines, and white-water rafting trips, and —"

"And probably people who lay out your towels for you? In case you're too tired to do it yourself?" I ask, squinting.

"Probably," Charlotte says, shrugging.

I groan out loud.

"Forget about that, Jules." Elinor says. "It's going to be the best summer ever, and you know it."

I know Elinor is trying to cheer me up, but all her cheerfulness makes me wonder what I'll do without her all summer.

"*¡Mi clase!*" Ms. Leon says now. "*¡A escribir!* To write!"

We get out our pencils. It's our last freewrite.

"What are your hopes and dreams for the summer? Tell me," Ms. Leon says, smiling at us. A lump of breakfast pops into my throat, which means there might be tears. I blink them away and start writing.

Things That Will Make This the Best Summer Ever:
1. I will not have to wear an orange-throw-up-colored

T-shirt every single day of
day camp because I will not be
at camp at all. Not even
one day.

2. I will spend time in Canada
   (that's another country!)
   filming all fifty-eight of my lines
   in *The Spy in the Attic* with
   former hockey star, now movie
   star Rick Hinkley and teen star
   Emma Saxony.

3. I will not mess up my lines and
   act like a doofus in front of
   big-time movie people Rick
   Hinkley and Emma Saxony.

Instead, I will become Lucy
Lamb, spy-girl.

4. I will be far, far away from
   Charlotte Stinkytown Pinkerton.
   For seven. Whole. Weeks.

5. And last, even though Elinor will
   be very far away, she will also
   be my first-ever pen pal!

My last list of second grade.

"Penceels down!" Ms. Leon says. Oh,
how I will miss her beachy voice!

When the bell finally rings, I feel only
one thing — relief! I made it through a
whole entire year of second grade with

Charlotte and the other fancy-pants ABC's (Abby and Brynn) and Teddy wish-he-was-a-teensy-bit-less-weird Lichtenstein. I had a big fat failure of a Swish commercial audition, filmed a whole episode of a brand-new sitcom, didn't miss out on our class moving-up play, and I even got a new best friend out of it. This was the best almost-worst year ever. And now, it is officially summer!

I meet my mom and Big Henry outside the school and we go to the park, where everyone is meeting for a last-day-of-second-grade picnic.

"They say your movie is going to be a blockbuster," Charlotte says the minute she sees me.

"Who says?" I say.

"*Variety*," Charlotte says.

"What's *Variety*?" I ask.

"It's a magazine all about important things that happen in show business," Charlotte says. "I can't believe you don't read it."

"Well, maybe Jules doesn't NEED a magazine to tell her things she already knows," Elinor says, "because she's an actual actress in an actual movie, so she already knows these things in the first place."

What am I ever going to do without Elinor this summer?

"Well, anyway, between Rick Hinkley and Emma Saxony, who is practically perfect, I don't think anyone will notice you so much, Jules, so that's good," Charlotte says.

"You won't have to be so crazy nervous all the time."

I glare at her because I'm pretty sure she isn't complimenting me.

"Anyway, have fun in England, Elinoh! Sorry you're missing my luncheon," Charlotte says before stomping away. She is throwing herself a going-to-sleepaway-camp luncheon at the diner. What makes it a luncheon and not just a lunch is the fact that it is a lunch party. I know this because I made the mistake of asking Charlotte when she invited me. "Oh, don't leave without giving me your address," she shouts from the swing set. "I'll be writing to you all on scented stationery with scented markers."

"She better not send me anything orange-scented," I say.

Maybe I don't read *Variety*, but I do know that this movie might end up being popular, and I am trying to forget about that since it makes me nervous. I have been trying to spend less time thinking about all these people going to sit in their sticky, squeaky movie-theater seats watching the spy version of me, and more time thinking about Canada and all the things I'm going to get to do there.

"She's wrong anyway, Julesium." Teddy Lichtenstein has arrived at the picnic. "According to research, any movie with a former sports star who tries to be a movie star doesn't end up doing very well at all."

"Thanks, Teddy," I say.

We run around and swing high on the swings and eat sushi rolls and grapes all afternoon until people start packing up. My mom and Teddy's mom, Andie, barely ever look up from the conversation they are having on our blanket, and I wonder why they never run out of things to talk about.

"Elinor," Mrs. Breedlove says, coming over to us, "we have to get on with it."

At this, my mom stands up and takes my hand and I know this means it's time to say good-bye.

"Well," Elinor says.

"Well," I say.

Mrs. Breedlove looks at the two of us just

staring at each other. "Well," she says in her very grown-up British way, "Mrs. Bloom and I have arranged for the two of you to e-mail each other whenever you want." She smiles a big grown-up smile when she says this.

Elinor and I jump up and down and scream-laugh at this news. "No stinky stationery for us!" Elinor says.

"Nope!" I say, and we give a quick hug while we're still laughing.

"Okay, off we go," Elinor's mom says, pulling her away.

"See you in August, Jules!" Elinor says.

"Write the second you get there," I say, and I turn away and start walking toward home, and fast. I have to shake off this feeling pronto, since there's nothing worse than saying good-bye to your still-brand-new best friend forever.

TAKE TWO

French-speaking Canada,
boys' names for girls, and other
things that are fishy

*Things I've Learned Since School Ended
Two Days Ago:*

1. On the way to my wardrobe
    fitting, I pictured myself as a
    paper doll being dressed in

special Lucy Lamb spy-girl clothes, complete with mini-binoculars, but when I got there I found out that Lucy Lamb might be an interesting character but she is NOT a very interesting dresser. For a spy-girl, Lucy Lamb wears a whole lot of not-so-spy-looking outfits.

2. Memorizing fifty-eight movie lines is harder than memorizing twelve spelling words for a Friday test. Much harder.

3. Mont-Tremblant is a very fancy-sounding French Canadian village where we will be filming the action scenes in the movie. To me, it sounds like a place from one of the fairy tales Grandma Gilda used to read me.

4. Coming up with an e-mail address is also hard. It took me three lists and one whole entire day of trying on someone else's clothes, but I suddenly thought of it in the cab on the way home and shouted it out loud to my mom and the cab driver.

"Supersecretspygirl!" I said, and my mom just looked at me and smiled.

5. Sometimes, things just hit you and that's that, like the smell of salmon.

We arrive home to my dad, who has been babysitting Big Henry while we were out all day and they have cooked us a dinner that makes the whole apartment stink.

I wrinkle my nose. "What?" he asks, smiling. "You don't like salmon anymore?"

"Too . . . hot . . . for . . . salmon," I say, fake choking.

"Save it for the movies, sister," my dad says. "Now go get all the city stuff off your hands and meet us at the island for supper." Most people in the world probably sit at a table to eat dinner, but we don't really have room for a table since we barely even have room for Big Henry. I guess it's an island because it kind of floats in the middle of our kitchen the way a tropical island floats in the middle of the ocean. So here we are, with the fish but without the palm trees.

I tell my dad about all the movie stuff of the day and recite some of my favorite lines, like, "Hold on a minute, am I a spy now?" I am supposed to say this with a furrowed brow, because that is what the script says to do. And that means I scrunch up my eyes like I'm trying to hold a pencil in between them. Big Henry laughs his head off when I do this.

By the end of dinner, my dad starts to talk in a British James Bond accent, which means it is time for me to go to my room to escape the smell and to practice my French. Ugly Otis follows me into my room, and I look at him and his ugly-cute, drooly face. "We are going to Canada, Ugly Otis, and not regular old English-speaking Canada. We are going to FRENCH-speaking Canada!" Otis is not excited by this news, but I am.

Before we go to the fancy-sounding village of Mont-Tremblant, we are all flying to a big city called Montreal on the day after my eighth birthday, which happens to be the day after America's birthday — my absolute two favorite days of the year. I had to get a passport and everything. So did Big Henry, and now I get butterflies in my stomach every time I think about all of the French kids playing on the playgrounds in French Canada saying French things as they swing from the monkey bars.

So far I only know how to say *"Je m'appelle Jules!"* and *"Bonjour!"* but I plan to spend the next week learning to say playground things like "Let's see if we can touch the sky with our feet!" and "Oh, don't mind my brother — he wears dinosaur rain boots no matter what!"

The phone rings, and I take off my "Learn to Speak French in a Week!" headphones to run to the kitchen to get it. I guess maybe I am hoping it's Elinor since I haven't heard from her yet and my dad's bad British accent made me really miss her perfect accent even more.

I pick up the phone. It isn't Elinor at all. It is Teddy's mom, Andie, whose name sounds like a boy's, but looks like a girl's. Again. I hand the phone to my mom.

"You already spoke to Andie three times today. What else could you possibly have to talk about?" I ask.

She shushes me and says, "Things."

"What kind of things?" I ask.

"None of your beeswax," she says.

"Something smells fishy," I say in my Lucy-Lamb-spy-girl voice. I also furrow my brow.

"Dinner," she says. "Dinner smells fishy. Now shoo."

I go ahead and shoo, but I hang out a bit in the hallway to see if I can overhear anything from their conversation. This is what Lucy Lamb does in the movie a few times,

according to the script. She *lurks*, which basically means she hangs out a little past when she is supposed to in order to spy. So this is what I do now. I lurk.

All I can hear are snippets of a boring conversation about what to pack for cool Canadian nights. I might as well plan my outfit for Stinkytown's going-away luncheon instead.

I start to lay out some clothes for our trip, too. In Montreal, we will film in a house where Lucy Lamb supposedly lives and where she has been left by her parents with a babysitter who is played by teenage star Emma Saxony. I think about Emma Saxony and think that her name is a name-up-in-lights type name. I was looking at her in a magazine one day when my mom told me she was the one playing Lucy Lamb's babysitter, and I almost fell off my chair. I've never met her, but her pizzazz practically jumped off the magazine page and onto the (not tropical) island where I was sitting.

The movie people hired me after seeing my messed-up audition for the Swish commercial. They told the casting director Colby Kingston that they needed a funny, New York–style kid for the role of Lucy Lamb. During all the movie meetings we've had over the last few days, everyone keeps reminding me that even though my role isn't that big, it is very important. I am the spoiler. To me that sounds like I am a Spider-Man villain who maybe sneaks into people's fridges and spoils their sliced turkey, but that's not what it means at all.

It means Lucy Lamb gets in everybody's way all the time and kind of ruins their plans. But by accident. Because Lucy's just this innocent little girl who only discovers things — like a spy in my attic! — by accident. So I guess when I, Jules Bloom, spit out all of that awful orangey Swish mouthwash and then *cha-cha-cha*ed, they thought they had hit the jackpot.

A few months ago, this would have made me very nervous and I would have pictured myself doing a terrible job of getting in the way of former hockey star, now movie star, Rick Hinkley. But after working on a sit-com, I am feeling a little bit more like the actress everyone thinks I am. Or at least I WAS before I found out one VERY important twist, which should have made the list of *Things I've Learned Since School Ended Two Days Ago*, but it deserves its OWN list.

Very Important Twists:

1. While I'm in Canada filming a movie with all these crazy-famous people, I will have to slide down a mudslide. And it's the very last scene of the movie,

which means I can't even get it
over with right away — the way
I always want to get my shot
first at the doctor's office.
That's it. That's the twist, and
it's a big one.

    I put down my pen and hide my list. I am
not going to think about this now. Right
now, I have packing to do, and we are
heading north — layers are in order!

bad news, worse news, and even worse news

"Everybody hustle!" Big Henry says.

We are standing on Broadway and all we have to do is cross the street and walk down one block and we will be at the diner. My favorite diner. It is the place where Colby Kingston overheard me singing my fizzy-milk jingle to Big Henry, which is how all this acting stuff got started in the first place. But it was my favorite place before that because it smells like turkey bacon and it has special salads with names like "Santa Fe" and "Field of Dreams." And even though I always, always, always get the same poached eggs on whole-wheat toast with home fries, I sometimes picture myself ordering a fancy salad instead. This Field-of-Dreams-salad-ordering person looks kind of the same in my head as a tall-icy-drink person.

"Nope," my mom says. "No need to hustle today, Hank."

"Why not?" Hank asks.

"Because we are on summer break," she says. My mom is taking time off this summer to be a real stay-at-home mom instead of working while we're at school and very late at night and is always huffing and puffing all around the apartment as a result. "This is what artists do," she says under her breath when she's sorting through our backpacks instead of finishing something she's working on in her studio. This makes me hope I never have to unpack a backpack in the middle of doing something else I want to be doing.

So I, for one, am very happy that there will be no huffing and puffing all summer long, and I'm also happy that none of us will be staying at home. "Let's stand on this corner and make a list, Julesie," my mom says.

"I don't have a pen," I say, feeling frantic and very excited to make a list while we are just standing on a street corner, waiting for the light to change. "Or paper!"

"It's okay," my mom says. "We're on summer break. 'No more teachers, no more books,'" she starts singing. Just like Elinor did. I laugh inside. "We'll just shout it out loud into the sky, and we'll remember because you always remember big, dramatic things."

"I'll remember," Hank says, and he closes his eyes tight. This is Big Henry's concentrating face. "Go."

"LIST OF THE THINGS WE LOVE ABOUT SUMMER BREAK!" my mom shouts.

I feel my face get red-hot and I look all around us. My mom is a little crazy, and I wish that I could be that kind of crazy, but I can't.

"I DON'T HAVE TO UNPACK ANY BACKPACKS!" she shouts again. "Your turn."

"I get to be Lucy Lamb!" I say, just a little louder than usual. This shouting thing is not for me.

"That wasn't exactly a shout, Jules, but it's okay," she says. "Hank?"

My brother keeps his eyes shut and yells, "I AM GOING TO CANADA AND I AM GOING TO LEARN TO SWIM!"

I look at my brother. Even though you might think he is a scrambled-eggs-and-chocolate-milk type person (because he loves scrambled eggs and chocolate milk more than anything), he is really not. He is a tall-icy-drink and Field-of-Dreams-salad person DISGUISED as a scrambled-eggs-and-chocolate-milk person. He gets this from my mom.

The shouting is finally over and we cross giant old Broadway without hustling as much as usual. I see Charlotte, Brynn, and Abby in the window of the diner, and they all start banging on the glass to say hi. When we walk in, I see that we are seated at the big corner booth. I love this table. It is giant and round and you can see out the window. You only get to sit there if you are a party of at least six, which means we

almost never get to sit there. For once, I am thankful for Charlotte and the fact that she is always throwing parties for herself.

I sit down between Brynn and an empty chair that I know is reserved for Teddy. The moms and Big Henry sit at the regular old four-person table next to us, which they connect to a little two-person table so that Henry and Charlotte's baby sister, Ella, can sit, too.

"Henry, will you babysit for me?" Mrs. Pinkerton says to my brother. "Ella loves big boys." I kind of wish I could babysit Ella. I only feel that way until she blows a raspberry and her mashed-up food sprays Big Henry in the face. He cracks up, and I turn back to my friends.

I listen to Brynn and Abby talk about their summer plans — Brynn is going to tennis camp and Abby is going to Europe.

"Like, England?" I ask.

"France and England!" Abby says. "Elinor even gave me her telephone number so that I can call her when we're in London."

Elinor didn't tell me this, which makes me feel bad, and when they finally put my poached eggs down in front of me, I don't feel like I can eat them. I can tell by the very hard pounding of my heart that this is the beginning of a very bad mood. Then, Teddy arrives, slamming himself into the seat next to me. He is way too close to me, so I can smell his mouthwash.

"Did you use Swish today?" I ask him.

"Yep," he says. "Sorry."

I cringe at this. The only thing that makes it okay that I am sitting next to the orange-fire-breathing best-friend-from-nursery-school monster is that he will be off to science camp in two days.

"Sorry about science camp," Brynn says to Teddy now.

I look at Teddy. "It's okay. They are going to reschedule it for later in the summer," he says.

"What happened?" I ask.

"There weren't enough kids for the first session," he says.

"So what are you gonna do instead?" Abby asks.

"Jules didn't tell you?" he asks.

I sense something terrible about to happen. "Tell them what?" I ask. "I don't know what you're talking about."

"We are going on a road trip with the Blooms, to Canada!" he says.

"No you're not," I say, pushing my chair away from the table. "We're flying there on an airplane. We have passports and my dad is taking time off from the restaurant and it is going to be perfect."

"Okaaaay," he says. "That's *not* what's happening."

Charlotte, Brynn, and Abby are all just staring at us, waiting.

I storm over to my mom, who is busy laughing with the other moms. Andie says, "Hi, kiddo."

I ignore her and turn face-to-face with my mom. "Why is Teddy telling everyone that we aren't flying to Canada and that we are going on a road trip instead . . . with the Lichtensteins?"

My mom looks at Andie. "You told him already?" she says.

"I had to. Science camp was canceled," Andie says.

"Jules, Andie and I thought it would be fun, since we have a few days to spare, if we all drove to Canada together. A road trip!" she says. "And we can celebrate your birthday on the road and we can stop and see some sights and then drive over the border to Canada. Pretty cool, right?"

"We don't even have a car," I say.

"We'll rent one," she says. "A super-cool one."

"You are going to be in a car with Teddy all the way to Canada?" Charlotte says now. "Oh. My. G —"

"Charlotte!" Mrs. Pinkerton says.

I don't wait for more. I slam my chair into the table and run out of the diner. My heart is pounding so hard now that it feels like it could fly right out of me and onto an *I Heart NY* tank top. I picture a real, thumping heart in place of the pretty love heart.

My mom interrupts my sidewalk day-dream. "Jules, come on. It's going to be fun. And Daddy will meet us there and —"

What? "Daddy isn't coming on the road trip?"

"No, he has so much to do for the restaurant opening. This will give him time to get things all set before he comes up for the movie shoot."

"So I won't be with Daddy on my birthday?" I ask. Now I'm going to cry.

"We will celebrate before we leave," she says. "Then Daddy and Teddy's father will fly up and meet us in Montreal. This is going to be fun, I promise. Now, you need to go back inside and eat your lunch and say a nice good-bye to your friends. Got it?"

"Fine," I say. I go back in, take one bite of my eggs, say my good-byes, and then I sit there in silence until it's time to leave.

"Have a great summer, Jules!" Charlotte says, hugging me. I can't even put my arms around her I am so mad. "Write me from Canada. Maybe just buy a postcard and spray it with something nice since you probably don't have scented stationery."

"No," I say. "I don't. Have a good time," I say to her and to Brynn and Abby.

"See you in two days!" Teddy says as we leave.

"Sure thing," I say.

I try to stay calm on the way home, but Henry is stepping on my heels and I just wish we could go back to where we were right before this awful luncheon, shouting all of our summer dreams into the air. But we can't.

TAKE FOUR

pre-birthday parties, fruity mail, and more things that stink

After a whole day and a whole night of sulking and feeling very, very bad for myself, I wake up to much better news.

"You have an e-mail, Jules," my mom says when I drag myself and my overlong pajamas into my seat at the kitchen island.

I feel lit up inside. Finally! "Lemme see!" I say, grabbing for her laptop.

But she pulls it away. "Nope, not until you promise to be enthusiastic about our road trip." She smiles at me like this is funny.

"You can't make someone feel something they don't feel," I say. This is what my mom always tells me.

"You can pretend," Big Henry says.

"That's true," my mom says. "You're an actress. *Pretend* to be happy about the road trip!"

We all laugh at this until I see . . . him.

"Hi, Julesie," my dad says.

"Hello," I say in a serious voice.

"You were just laughing," he says. "I saw you!"

"I was," I say. "At Mommy and Big Henry."

"So, you're over your tantrum," he says. I do not like when he says *tantrum* because it makes me sound like a giant baby.

"It wasn't a tantrum," I say. "I was just mad. And I am not finished being mad at you."

He sits down and rubs my back. "But today is your pre-birthday party!" He says. "And for your present, you will get a special sneak peek at the BLOOM kitchen, where we will bake a cake — just you and me."

This sounds so wonderful I cannot hold in the not-mad feelings for one more second. I burst into his hug. "Can it be chocolate? Can we use coffee in it?" My dad's special chocolate cake has coffee inside and delicious white icing.

"Decaf," he says.

"Yeth!" Hank says. "I mean, yes." He really is working very hard at his speech therapy.

I run toward my room to get ready until I remember something. I run back to the kitchen, where my mom is holding out her laptop. Elinor's e-mail!

"Hey, how did she get my e-mail address, anyway?" I ask.

"I sent it to her mom as soon as you told me what you wanted it to be," she says with a wink. My mom has a way of making up for her road-tripping ways very, very quickly.

I open up the e-mail from iheartlondon@
pizzazzorama.com. I am right away very
jealous of her e-mail address. It's a good one.

Dear SUPERSECRETSPYGIRL:

I made it all the way to London and my dad was waiting
for us at the airport and he told me that he is taking the
whole month off just to be with me and take me all
around! Isn't it wonderful?

Well, I miss you already and was thinking that since I
am in London, where James Bond is from – Do you
know who that is? He is the most famous spy ever,
Jules, and maybe Lucy Lamb will be like him! – that
maybe I will give you your spy assignments over
e-mail the way James Bond gets assignments in his
movies. Yes? Tell me yes and I will write you back. And

also tell me all the wonderful things you are doing without me.

Love,

Elinor

I look up at my mom. "Can I write her back right away?"

"Of course!" she says.

Dear Elinor,

I love your e-mail address and your idea, so yes, please give me assignments!

You will never guess what happened. I am going on a road trip to Canada with Teddy and his mom and my mom and Big Henry, and I found all of this out at Charlotte's good-bye luncheon, and now I have to be in a car on

my birthday. And do you think Teddy is going to throw
up in the car? I do.

Now, what is my assignment? I wish my real name were
Lucy Lamb, don't you?

Have fun with your dad and don't miss me too much!

Love,

Jules (SUPERSECRETSPYGIRL)

I close the laptop. My pen-pal summer
has begun! I run down the hall to get
dressed for making a special pre-birthday
cake at my dad's new restaurant, which is
going to open the minute we all get back
from Canada!

"What do you want for your birthday
dinner?" my dad asks me from the hallway.

"Brisket," I say.

"Brisket?" he asks. "As in, Grandma Gilda–style brisket?"

"Yup," I say.

"That's not exactly a July food, Jules," my dad says.

"It's my favorite food," I say.

"Brisket it is," he says.

I smile. Brisket and chocolate cake and pen-pal e-mail from Elinor. This is a pretty good pre-birthday day so far.

Later, after I pick out all of the most important things for my trip — cozy pajamas, my pillow, my notebook, and my script — my dad and I leave my mom and Big Henry to finish packing. This makes me nervous because I keep picturing us getting to Canada and realizing that the only things in the suitcase are rubber ducks and paintbrushes and dinosaur rain boots.

But I feel all better the second we arrive at BLOOM. Outside it looks like a farmer's market, and inside it smells like fresh construction and cilantro. "We should have named the restaurant Fresh," I say to my dad, since that's what it smells like and since the restaurant is only going to serve fresh, organic food.

"I like BLOOM," he says. I like it, too. I named it! We get right to baking and I get to wear an apron and prepare the ingredients and make hot decaf coffee, which makes the batter smell especially good as it churns and splashes inside the giant mixer. I look at the hot chocolatey stew and think about the mudslide part of the movie, which has been worrying me. It seems like it would be fun, but I keep thinking of how sticky and disgusting it will be, and will it get in my mouth and stuck inside my ears and toes? Will I be able to breathe? Suddenly, I picture myself swirling around inside the mixer along with all that chocolate and hot decaf coffee and —

"Jules!" my dad says loudly.

"What?" I say. Then I snap out of it and see batter flying everywhere — hitting the wall of the kitchen and hitting my dad and me smack in the face!

I scream and my dad turns off the mixer fast, but he is laughing hysterically. I start to laugh, too, and we sit there for a while wiping ourselves down and waiting for the laugh to wear off. Then my dad pops up and gets the un-flung batter into the cake pan and into an oven. In the other oven is my birthday brisket — it smells so good I can taste it. We spend some time cleaning up, and then we set one of the tables for dinner.

As I am folding the napkins, my dad asks, "What were you thinking about when the batter went flying?"

"Nothing," I say. I don't really want anyone to know that I am afraid about filming the movie. I've wanted to make this movie since the day Colby called to say I didn't get the Swish commercial. Plus, everyone is used to me being nervous about things like orange-flavored mouthwash, or having to act like a sassy little sister, and singing on countertops, so now I just want everyone to think that, for once, I am not nervous. Not about Emma Saxony and not about a giant mud pit that will probably swallow me up and spit me back out like some bad-tasting mud mouthwash.

"Nothing at all?" my dad asks.

"Nope. Well, okay, I was thinking about how much fun that mudslide scene is going to be," I say.

"Are you nervous about it?" he asks.

"Nope," I lie. This is a good lie, I think. Now my dad doesn't have to worry about me being nervous without him and he can just concentrate on the restaurant and meeting us in Canada. It's a helpful lie.

"Wow, good," he says.

My mom and Big Henry walk in then, and my dad says, "Wait a minute. Jules, close your eyes."

I do. And when I open them, the restaurant is dark except for lots of candles on

our table and little white lights
lit up all around us.

"Happy pre-birthday, Julesie,"
my dad says, handing me
a newspaper-wrapped
present. I open it, and it
is a compass. On the back
it says, *To find your way! Love, Dad.*

I hug him very tight and my mom puts
on music, and we all sit and eat brisket and
carrots and potatoes and chocolate cake,
and then we clean up and lock up and walk
home as a family. It is the greatest last-night-
before-the-big-road-trip night ever.

We check the mail in the lobby when we
get home and there is something for me —

pink mail. Strawberry-scented mail. She just left today and already I have mail from her. I open it up.

Dear Jules,

Hopefully you are getting this before you leave for your road trip. I can't believe you will be spending so much time with Teddy — with all of his throwing up. Yuck! Maybe it will help your acting.

What is your e-mail? Mine is strawberryscentedcharlotte@ pizzazzorama.com. Even though I have not left for camp yet, I just know it will be great, and I'm planning on starring in the camp show and everything so maybe I'll finally give you some real acting competition.

I'm not even nervous about being away all summer. Maybe I'll even get the same bunk as Emma Saxony. . . .

Bon voyage! (That's French for "have a good trip.")

Charlotte

Even though I don't care AT ALL that Charlotte is going to be in a camp play and even though I would NEVER, EVER want to be away from my whole family all summer, I feel that heart-thumping feeling I get when I am mad about something. It seems like Charlotte is saying I'm not very good at acting, and she's probably right, but it makes me mad anyway.

I picture Charlotte being perfect in her camp play and everyone clapping really loud for her in their *Camp Lackahanna* sweatshirts and hats and then toasting her with giant pitchers of bug juice, which is just fruit punch, but at camp they call fruit punch bug juice. All of this seems more glamorous than being in Canada and sliding down a mudslide.

I write back to her immediately from my mom's computer.

Dear strawberryscentedcharlotte,

Your stationery is very smelly. My e-mail address is

SUPERSECRETSPYGIRL@pizzazzorama.com, and no, I haven't started my road trip yet, so Teddy has not thrown up yet. If he does I will let you know and you will be very glad that I am not sending you actual stationery since I will be locked in a car with him and his throw up! Maybe Teddy's e-mail should be throwupscentedteddy@ pizzazzorama.com.

Have a good summer!

Jules

I hit SEND and feel bad right away that I made fun of Teddy like that. He hasn't thrown up in a very long time, and he's funny and smart, but sometimes his weirdness freaks people out and I'm afraid they will think I'm weird, too, because I spend so much time with him. I try not to think about the e-mail I sent Charlotte, and instead I concentrate on saying good-bye to my room.

There is a knock at my door. It's my dad. "Seems like a special assignment has come in, Agent Bloo — I mean, Agent Lamb." He hands me the computer.

SUPERSECRETSPYGIRL: Special assignment from London. Practice stealth. Don't be afraid to get help from strangely scientific nursery-school friends and little brothers in giant rain boots.

E

I close the laptop and look at my dad. "What's stealth?" As soon as I ask this, I think he is going to tell me to figure it out myself, since this is what my dad is famous for, but for some reason, he doesn't.

Instead, he peeks around the curtain that divides my half of the bedroom from Big Henry's, and then looks back at me, putting his finger to his lips in a shushing way. Then

he gets down on his hands and knees and crawls slowly through the curtain and toward my brother, who is reading *Hop on Pop* to Ugly Otis in his bed. I follow my dad on tiptoes, trying not to laugh. My dad gets really close to Big Henry then, and pops his head up at my brother and says, "Boo!" Well, Big Henry practically leaps out of his pajamas, and I start to laugh so hard I barely notice that Ugly Otis has come over to drool on me.

My dad stands up. "That's stealth," he says, and he walks out of the room. And Big Henry and Ugly Otis and I all laugh ourselves silly until bedtime.

TAKE FIVE

pileups, racing stripes, and in-car entertainment

It takes us all morning to leave the city, even though my mom told us we had to get up at "the crack of dawn" so we could get a good start. Teddy and Big Henry and I all wait in the lobby of our building, sitting on top of loads of suitcases, waiting for the moms to arrive with our rental car.

"Teddy, quick, behind the mail wall," I say.

Teddy pops off of the duffel bag he was sitting on and runs to hide behind the mail wall.

"Hank," I say, trying to get my brother to be part of our stealth mission.

"What, Julth?" Big Henry whisper-yells.

I look over at the mail wall Teddy is hiding behind. "I only answer to 'Jules,'" I say, trying to get him to correct his lisp. I am worried that if he still has a lisp when he gets to kindergarten, he will be made fun of, and I do NOT want that to happen, so I am helping.

It is silent for a minute.

"What, Jules?" Big Henry says. Properly this time.

"We are being spies. Come and practice," I say.

I hide behind the wall with them and we all crouch down, peeking around the corner. "What are we spying on?" Teddy asks.

"We are on the lookout for a minivan," I say.

"Ah," he says. "Should be another three to four minutes, according to my math."

I picture a minivan taxi pulling up with my mom as the taxi driver and a little TV in the back that tells us the weather and shows us celebrity interviews and Swish mouth-wash commercials. And this makes me think about John McCarthy, the Swish boy, who also played my brother on *Look at Us Now!*, which makes me wonder if we will get to make more episodes since I loved being Sylvie and being with my sitcom siblings.

Right now, my real-life sibling is climbing up my back for a good look at the curb. We are all in a huddle, trying to remain unseen like good spies. Suddenly, we see it. It is red, it has a racing stripe, and it is HUGE.

"Oh . . . my . . ." Teddy says.

I can tell what is about to happen, because when Big Henry sees a giant car with a racing stripe on the side, well —

"Lemme out! Lemme

through!" he says, pushing out of our little huddle so hard that we all go flying toward the entrance to our building, landing in a pile at my mom's feet.

"Well, well, well," my mom says, looking at us and at Joe the doorman. "Looks like they're excited after all."

I am laughing so hard I cannot stand up, and Big Henry is still trying to push his way over us and toward the big car, and with every one of his footsteps on my back I laugh harder and I can't get up and all I can hear is Teddy saying "I can't breathe!" from underneath me, but he is laughing, too.

Finally, Big Henry makes his way to the sidewalk outside, and he starts jumping up and down, and finally, Teddy and I can stand up. My mom takes a picture of us as we recover from our collapse, and then she takes about a hundred more as we admire and explore our minivan — or, as I will now call it, our MAXI-van.

"Told you it would be cool," my mom says to me.

I shake my head at her. She's one of the craziest people I know!

We say our good-byes to Joe, who helps get everything in the car, and we buckle up. "Bon voyage," Joe says, and I cringe. This reminds me of Charlotte, and the fact that I have not practiced one word of French in days. I have also not practiced my lines for the movie or my spy acting, and we are three days away from filming. Here come the butterflies.

I distract myself by writing a "mission-kind-of-accomplished" e-mail to Elinor. *Stealth has been practiced,* I write. *Ended up in a heap in the lobby of our building. Need more practice. Ready for next assignment.* I hand my mom her phone and see that Teddy looks nervous.

"Uh, Mom," Teddy says, holding out both of his wrists.

Andie looks at him and gasps. "Don't worry, don't worry — I've got 'em!" She is digging in her giganto purse for something. *What could it be?* I wonder. I see her pull out bags of chips, and then gum, and then DVDs, and chargers, and candy, and at last she hoists two little wristbands in the air.

"Phew!" Teddy says, grabbing them from her. I stop spying and look straight at him.

"What are those?" I ask.

"Sea-Bands," he says, like this is a perfectly normal thing to say. Like any old person would just know what these strange things are that he is putting on his wrists. "They keep me from feeling dizzy in the car."

"How do they do that?" I ask. I do not for one second believe that bracelets can keep a person from being dizzy.

"They put acupressure on the points on

your wrists that trigger nausea and vomiting," he says.

I do not understand one word of that.

"Acupressure?" I ask. "Is that a science word?"

"Kind of," he says.

I squint at him and notice that we are not even on the highway yet and Teddy is looking a little green. I look out the window and pray to the George Washington Bridge that the bands really do work.

"Let's watch *Ramona and THE Beezus!*" Big Henry says, and I snort so loud the whole car starts laughing.

"What?" he asks, laughing anyway since Big Henry always likes to be in on the joke.

"Nothing," I say. I don't want him to know that the movie is called *Ramona and Beezus*, and not *Ramona and* THE *Beezus*, because then he might correct it the way he corrects his lisp when I remind him. And I only ever want him to say it his way.

We watch a movie in the maxi-van and ride a good long way before we have to stop for a bathroom break. When we get out, I stretch and shake out all the snack crumbs.

Then I beg my mom to check my e-mail, and she does.

"Here you go," she says, handing me her very smart phone.

SUPERSECRETSPYGIRL:

Assignment: Be sure not to let on that you are a tourist. There is nothing that annoys people more than tourists – even in Plattsburgh. Come up with a reason why you might be spending the night in Plattsburgh, and especially on your birthday. This is your second spy mission. Mission: You Are Not a Tourist in Plattsburgh.

Love,

E

P.S. It's true that sometimes stealth missions end up in a heap.

P.P.S. Happy birthday! I know it's tomorrow, but I wanted to be first.

I smile because I know she thinks our stealth heap was funny, and I smile because she remembered my birthday *and* because she didn't say "Happy Fourth of July," since she probably doesn't think it's a happy thing, being from England! I give my mom her phone back, then I prepare for Plattsburgh and the mission that lies ahead.

TAKE SIX

human birthday presents, undercover waffle-making, and the flight pattern of ducks

We are in Plattsburgh. It was a terrible night. I missed the Fourth of July fireworks and I don't even remember getting here. I just remember the bright lights of the lobby and too-loud elevator noises, and then I remember getting into a big double bed and my mom and Big Henry getting into another big double bed right next to mine. But Hank did not stay put for one minute. He fell out of bed three hundred times, and I was so sad about waking up in Plattsburgh on my birthday, it took me forever to fall back to sleep every single time.

I rub my eyes and see that it is 8:30 a.m., which might be the latest Hank and my mom have ever slept. They are morning people. I am a night owl, and so is my dad. There is a knock on the door and I don't know if I should get it. My mom and Big Henry are still sound asleep. There is another knock, but this time there is a voice attached to the knock.

"Is there an Eddie Bloom in there?" it says.

My heart leaps! It's Grandma Gilda! I fling open the door.

"George!" I say, and I throw my arms around her waist. We stay like that for a good minute before Big Henry joins us.

"Mommy!" he shouts. "Grandma Gilda is in Platthburgh." He looks at me. "Plattsburgh." I smile.

"Did she give you the card?" my mom asks from the bed.

I look at my grandma Gilda and she hands it to me.

Dear Julesie,

Since I cannot be with you on your real birthday, I sent this crazy lady to entertain you in my absence. Happy birthday!

Love,

Dad

"Does he call me a crazy lady in that note?" George asks. "Lemme see!"

"Nope," I say. "It's mine, all mine."

This is shaping up to be an okay birthday after all.

We head downstairs and I remember immediately that I am not supposed to be acting like a tourist, so I walk with confidence (this is the kind of thing they write on movie scripts) over to the make-your-own waffle maker. They have a make-your-own waffle maker! I duck behind a counter to watch others make THEIR own waffles first, since I must look like I know what I am doing if I am going to look like I belong here.

"Hi," a little kid says to me while I'm still in ducking position. The little kid is not Big Henry.

"Hi," I say.

"I am from Westchester," he says. "Why are you hiding?"

"I'm not hiding," I say. "I'm tying my shoe." Good one!

"We are on our way to Canada. Where are you from?" he asks.

"I'm from right here in Plattsburgh," I lie. I mean, I pretend.

"Then why are you staying in a hotel?" he asks. Here it is, my big moment.

"Oh, well, it's my birthday today so we're having my celebration luncheon here at the hotel — what with the make-your-own waffles and all."

"Oh," he says, and then he shuffles off to his parents.

I did it! He definitely believes me.

Big Henry meets me at the waffle maker and I scoop out some batter like I saw the other people do. I see Big Henry's eyes get big and wide and I glop it onto the griddle thing. I put some extra batter in then, since I like how Big Henry is looking at me and I want to make his eyes get even wider. I am a very good make-your-own-waffle maker.

Then I say, "Do you want to do the honors, Big Henry?" This is what my dad says when we cook together and he lets me turn on a mixer or something.

"Yes!" he says. I hoist him up a little and he slams the top griddle thingy onto the bottom griddle thingy, and we both end up with a whole lot of batter all over our faces.

"Batter splatter!" I say, and we crack up while we wait for the waffles to be ready.

"What's all the cackling about?" Grandma Gilda asks. She is suddenly at our level, all scrunched down into a squat. We are face-to-face with George. She takes a finger to Big Henry's face and wipes the batter off. Then she licks her finger!

"Mmmm," she says. "I love batter splatter." Then we laugh all over again, and finally our waffles are ready and we sit down to eat my birthday breakfast in Plattsburgh.

"Julesium," Teddy says from the other side of the table, "is this your birthday party?"

"I guess so," I say.

"So I am the only friend who was invited?" he asks, smiling.

"Yep," I say. I guess he is.

"You can have a friend party later in the summer, Julesie. Maybe even at BLOOM!" my mom says as she and Andie join us at the table.

"Ooooh," I say. I didn't even think of that. We will have our own restaurant when we get home. Then this makes me miss my dad, thinking of him working while we're here eating waffles and road-tripping.

Big Henry interrupts my sad thought to give me a present. It is wrapped in a hand towel from the hotel bathroom. I open it up and before my eyes I see Big Henry's most prized possession. It is a rubber duckie with a mask on.

"You're giving me Bat Duck?" I ask. Hank has one million rubber duckies, but this one is his favorite. I look at my mom and she shrugs.

"Yeth," he says. "Well, you can just borrow him for your birthday."

I am relieved. "Thanks, Hank," I say.

It is a rainy Fifth of July, and it turns out there isn't much to do in Plattsburgh, so we decide to go for a swim in the rooftop indoor swimming pool! We are going to try to teach Big Henry to swim.

I bring Bat Duck, thinking this will help Hank feel more confident. And it smells like a nice warm bath in the pool area, so that should help, too. Teddy and I both cannonball into the deep end and then we swim back to the shallow end, where Big Henry is in his swim vest and his goggles, clinging to the wall. I stand a little bit apart from him and tell him to swim to Bat Duck and me.

"Bat Duck is waiting for you!" I say.

"Bat Duck is drowning," Teddy says now. Then he dunks Bat Duck under the water and lets him go flying into the air. I laugh as Bat Duck flies over our heads and think this is a good idea Teddy has.

Hank does NOT agree. "Hey!" he says. "Stop it."

"Sorry," Teddy says. "I was just trying to get you to save him. I'll go get him." Teddy swims away and I walk toward Big Henry.

"Come on," I say. "I'll hold your hands just like Daddy does."

"Stop being bossy!" Big Henry says to me. "I won't swim till Daddy comes."

"Hank," I say, annoyed that he called me bossy, "won't it be fun to surprise Daddy when he gets to Mont-Tremblant?"

"No," he says. He will not let go of that wall. His little fingers hang on tight. I give up, which makes me feel like a big old failure on my eighth birthday.

We dry off after a while and head back to our rooms. "Jules," Teddy whispers at me in the elevator, "I couldn't find Bat Duck."

I whip my head around and stare at him. Then I put my finger to my lips. We cannot let Big Henry find out. Our moms want us all to get showered and ready to go when we get back to the rooms, so I have to think fast. My mom and Big Henry get bath stuff together and I hear them turn the water on in the bathroom.

"George," I whisper once I don't think they can hear, "we have a problem."

"Every problem has a solution, Eddie." This is one of George's positive affirmations.

I tell her about Bat Duck. "Doesn't he have a million of those ducks?" she asks.

"Yes," I say, "but only one Bat Duck."

"Give me a black marker and a duck," she says. I laugh at this and so does George. I get her the black marker quickly and feel more like a spy than ever. I can't wait to tell Elinor.

I watch George draw a bat mask across the face of one of Hank's rubber ducks, then we nod at each other. It is done. I sneak past my mom and Hank at the sink and toss it into the pile of duckies sitting by the bathtub, and then we wait.

"This is not Bat Duck," Big Henry says from the bath.

"Jules!" my mom yells.

I look at George and she shrugs. "Make it a good story," she says. "An adventure."

I tell my mom and Hank what happened, and my brother takes the news pretty well. Especially since my mom promises to ask

the woman at the hotel desk to send Bat
Duck to us if they find him.

"WHEN they find him," I remind her. I
feel terrible.

In the lobby, we sit on our suitcases again
until Andie pulls the car around. I am
sad because I haven't heard from Elinor or
my dad.

"Check this out," Grandma Gilda says.
She is holding one of her gossipy Hollywood
magazines, and the one and only Emma

Saxony is on the
cover. She is wear-
ing big sunglasses.
I look away.

"What is it?"
George asks.

"Nothing," I say. I don't want to say that Emma makes me nervous, which she does.

"I can see why you're nervous," Teddy says. "She's beautiful. Like, science beautiful."

"What does that mean?" I ask. "And I'm not nervous."

"It means it's a fact," he says.

"Says here she is releasing her first song this week," George reports.

"Great," I say. She can sing, too.

"That could be you one day, Eddie," she says. "Isn't that crazy?"

"Mom," my mom says, "stop." I love when my mom calls George "Mom." I sometimes forget that she's her mom's kid.

"Fine," George says. "Just saying . . ."

We all pile in the car, where we drive and
drive, and then where we sit and sit and sit
at the border. For hours.

*Things That Make It Better to Sit at the
Border:*

1. My dad calls and sings "Happy
   Birthday" and says he and
   Teddy's dad will meet us in Mont-
   Tremblant in two days, which
   seems like a long time from now,
   but it still cheers me up.

2. I write Elinor a loooong e-mail
   about waffles in Plattsburgh,

losing Bat Duck, and then
painting another duck's face
and sneaking around.

3. Teddy and I tell Big Henry a
story called "The Adventures of
Bat Duck," which begins when
Bat Duck goes flying out of the
indoor pool in Plattsburgh.
Turns out, he landed on the roof
of a truck headed for Canada
and he's getting into all kinds of
trouble along the way. Even
George and Andie and my mom
chime in, and Big Henry loves
every second of it.

We are getting closer and closer to the border, which makes me feel farther and farther from home, and this makes me panic about a whole bunch of things at once. Another list, a list of Things That Are Making Me More Nervous as We Sit Here Doing Nothing (a list I am only writing in the first place because it is the only thing to do while sitting at the border):

1. Elinor hasn't written all day, which maybe means she is having a perfect time being home and has forgotten all about me. And maybe her parents are going to work things out and then she will never come back.

2. I can't stop thinking about Charlotte's fancy acting camp. I never went to acting camp, and even at my own day camp I never wanted to perform with my group in our

end-of-summer show. I still
mostly like performing for my
brother and our stuffed
animals, with a flashlight for a
microphone.

3. Tomorrow is day one of being a
real live movie actress, and I
think it maybe would have been
a good idea to go to acting
camp before agreeing to this.

voilà! concierge! (and other words I didn't know were French)

We finally get to Montreal very late in the night, and I am still mad that my dad's not here and that I haven't heard back from Elinor, which means she's probably having a grand old time in London and maybe Abby is even there by now and they're off having a grand old time together and forgetting all about me and forgetting my birthday.

Teddy and Big Henry are asleep when we arrive at the hotel, so my mom tells me to come inside with her to check in while Andie starts to get the boys awake enough to get to our rooms.

There are beautiful city lights all around and a red carpet going into the hotel entrance and a café on the street with peo-ple clinking glasses and music playing loudly. It feels a little bit like New York City except for one thing. NO ONE is speaking English! It's crazy. I mean, we DROVE here from New York. It isn't like we got on an airplane and flew all the way to Paris or something. I am staring at everyone when my mom yanks my arm toward the lobby.

"Bonjour!" the woman behind the counter says.

"Bonjour," my mom says. Her accent doesn't sound like that woman's accent and I feel embarrassed for her.

I just say "hi" to the woman and not "bonjour," since I don't want to sound like a tourist. I hear people speaking French all around me and it makes me nervous not to know what they are saying. The woman produces our room keys, which look like credit cards, and says, "Voilà!" I smile because I know what that means. Suddenly I forget all about border traffic and Elinor forgetting my actual birthday and I forget about being nervous and I feel very excited instead — about being in Canada and about being in a real live movie!

It is much too early to be awake, but my mom and I are on our way to the set of the movie, which is just outside a house in Old Montreal. I have brought all my New York butter-flies with me and they are flitting around in my stomach like crazy.

I try not to think about how nervous I am to be with movie stars and to slide down mudslides, because I am really trying not to be nervous-Jules. I want to be confident-Jules.

There are big trailers lined up on the street when we arrive, and a big tent with tons of food that all looks very delicious. I would really want to eat it if my belly wasn't making sounds so loud I could hardly hear.

"Yoo-hoo!" Colby Kingston's voice somehow manages to be louder than my rumbling stomach.

"Colby!" my mom says, and they hug and kiss, and then Colby hugs and kisses me, too.

"I didn't know you would be here," I say.

"Wouldn't miss it," she says. Colby's smile twinkles when she says this, and she just reminds me of magic. I am very happy she's here with us.

"Ready to meet your co-stars?" Colby asks. She takes my hand in hers and I stare at her perfectly polished nails until we arrive at Rick Hinkley's trailer.

Even though I got to meet Rick Hinkley a few months ago, back when we were supposed to do the movie the first time, I am more nervous than ever, and I wish I were anywhere but here, on the stoop outside this very famous man's pretend house.

"Hi there, ladies!" A booming voice comes out of Rick Hinkley's body. He has opened the door himself, which I think is funny. I was picturing some assistant-type person with a clipboard answering the door and making us wait a long time to see him. But it's just Rick, in jeans and a T-shirt. "You must be Jules," he says. "I mean, you must be Lucy Lamb."

I am surprised he knows my real name and my pretend name, since I only have a couple of lines and I'm a nobody compared to him and Emma Saxony. I feel my face get hot and I don't dare say anything since those butterflies might just fly out like orange-flavored Swish, all over the place, which is, after all, what got me into this mess in the first place. I decide to nod.

"So you're the kid who gets me into a pile of mud, huh?" he says. For some reason, he sounds nervous to me.

I shrug, and as soon as I do, I feel mad at

myself for shrugging. I thought I had gotten over all of that during the sitcom. I take a deep breath. "I guess I am," I say.

"It's okay, I forgive ya," he says. Then everyone kind of fake laughs and I feel a little better. Rick Hinkley doesn't seem like a movie star, really. He just seems like a regular goofy dad-type guy.

Next stop, Emma Saxony. "So, Jules," Colby says, knocking on the trailer door of Emma Saxony, "ready to meet your babysitter?"

I take a deep breath, and this time it isn't the star who opens the door. It is the star's assistant, holding the star's little dog. "Hi, hi, hi," she says. "We're a little busy right now. Jules? Nice to meet you. I'm sure you and Emma will get along great. I'll let her know you came."

The whole time the assistant is talking I can only look at the back of Emma Saxony's head. She is getting her makeup done and talking on her phone, and I can just about see her eyes in the mirror. Her sparkly, blue-green, teen-idol, megastar eyes. And she is laughing a big, grown-up-sounding laugh into her phone and I can't hear anything else but her laugh. She is like a magnet, pulling me off of the trailer stoop, under the armpit of the chatty assistant, around the tail of the yapping dog, and into the bright makeup lights of the coolest room I've ever seen. I have ducked around every-one who was trying to keep me from the

star and while they try to figure out how
to deal with the situation, I admire the
turquoise-and-cream wallpaper, the sparkly
chandelier hanging overhead, the music
filling the air around me. It is Emma

Saxony's voice I hear singing. She is listening to her own song.

"Who is that?" I hear her say, and I realize she is talking about me. "Is that a fan who got in here somehow? Someone help

me!" she says, and she stands up with her hair still clipped up and toilet-paper-type tissue sticking out from her robe.

"Oh —" I start to say. "I'm not a fan — Well, I mean, I'm a fan, but I'm also —"

"Help me! Help me!" she screams, and then the assistant comes running toward us, and the little yapping dog goes crazy and jumps out of the assistant's arms, then runs through my legs, making me lose my balance and I go flying. Flying! Right into Emma Saxony, and we both fall down.

So there I am, lying on top of megastar teen idol Emma Saxony and her big, poofy megastar bathrobe! And I don't even think about being embarrassed. Well, I do think about that, and I am that, but what I also think is that Charlotte would just plain fall over if she saw this.

"Jules!" my mom says, trying to pick me up. There is a barking little dog on my back that needs to be picked up first, though.

"Get her off of me," Emma Saxony yells. "Now!"

"Emma," I hear Colby say now, in her nice, calm Colby way. "This is Jules Bloom. She will be playing Lucy Lamb. She is your co-star and I brought her over to meet you. Remember?"

Emma looks up at the ceiling like her memory might be hanging out up there instead of inside her head where it belongs. "Um, yes, sure. I remember. Hi, Jules. Nice to meet you. Next time, knock." She says all of this in a very fake voice and looks at her assistant while she speaks and not at me. Not once.

I can't believe how much I don't like her. My heart is doing all the pounding it usually does in situations like this one, but I don't think it is because I am nervous. I think it is because I am mad. I drove all the way to Canada, on my birthday, without my dad. For this! I run past everyone and burst outside and find an Old Montreal curb to sit on. It stinks because of all the Old Montreal horse and buggies everywhere and I am right at nose level of the stink. I make a list, sitting there.

Reasons I Wish I Never Came to Canada:

1. Emma Saxony now thinks I am a complete doofus, which I don't even really care about since she isn't even a little bit nice.

2. I don't speak French and everyone around me does, which makes me feel shy and twists my stomach into knots.

3. The horse and buggies make me think of Central Park, and that feels very, very far away.

4. I miss Elinor, who would definitely know the exact right thing to make me feel better about the Emma Saxony situation right now, if she would even remember to write to me at all!

5. Being in Canada is making me wish I were at camp instead. I'd even wear an orange T-shirt right now.

Then the doors to the trailer burst open, and out walks Emma Saxony, and she is dressed and has sunglasses on, and camera flashes go off everywhere around me. I can't even see, there are so many of them. Where did all those cameras come from?

Emma walks over to me and holds out both of her hands to help me up. I have no choice but to take them and smile.

"Sorry about that, Jules," she says. "All morning in makeup makes me cranky. How about we get a chai latte?"

I have no idea what a chai latte is or why there are so many people taking my picture. All I know is that Emma Saxony is smiling and GLOWING and laughing and I am not. And of course, this makes me nervous. Really nervous. Because how am I supposed to have any pizzazz at all if she's got ALL of it?

TAKE EIGHT

mouth exercises, teen-idol insults, and the lost art of shrugging

Luckily, our chai-latte time is short since I had to meet with my acting coach, who makes me open my mouth very wide, and we work on my expressions and on something called *enunciating*. It's a big word people use when they could just say "speak clearly." While I'm busy doing this, Emma and Rick and a bunch of other people start filming. Right away, just like that. Then the director comes in to tell us he's "liking the light and the vibe" and wants me to start filming my scenes today!

The good news is, I only have a few lines in the Montreal part — whiny lines like, "But Mommy always lets me stay up late on Saturday nights" and "If you take that call, I'm just going to watch more TV. . . ." I'm just a little girl Emma babysits the night of the big heist she's trying to stop from happening. I am the spoiler — I get the real movie stars into trouble they wouldn't have otherwise gotten into.

Lucy Lamb is very smart and very observant. Quickly, she understands that Emma Saxony is no run-of-the-mill babysitter. (*No kidding*, I think!) Lucy figures this out by listening to Emma's phone conversations. This is when I have to say in a whisper voice (which I practice over and over with my acting coach), "She's no babysitter; she's a spy."

After a very long time getting my makeup done (you need a LOT of makeup just to look like a regular eight-year-old girl in a movie), it is my turn to be a movie actress!

"Jules," the director says, "here we go! Action!"

So we film all these house scenes in this cool house that is nothing like the *Look at Us Now!* townhouse on the Upper East

Side. It is old and creaky and a little messy downstairs, but upstairs in the attic, it is something else completely! There is a spy living in the attic. Lucy's eyes practically pop out of her head when she sees super-crazy modern computers and lights that make her attic look like a Star Wars movie. And, plus, right there in front of her is Rick Hinkley, and he's talking to HER babysitter on the phone. Lucy was right!

This is where I get to make this super-funny expression. I am supposed to open my mouth real big like I

am going to scream, but then I have to put one of my hands and then the other hand over my OWN mouth to shush myself, and then stumble backward and fall, which makes Rick realize I've found them out. They say this is called "physical comedy," and I think it is the thing I am the BEST at. EVERYONE laughs when I do it. Everyone except Emma Saxony.

And then, since I am Lucy Lamb and not Jules Bloom, and since Lucy is a bored little girl who wants more adventure in her life (this is what the script says), Lucy gets involved in the spy mission! Lucy's parents are running late so fake-sitter Emma makes a snap decision and she tells Lucy they have to make a run for it, and from there, Lucy gets to go with her and Rick Hinkley on the next leg of their adventure.

After all these scenes, I am feeling more and more like Lucy Lamb, and as we climb out of the back window and onto the street, I see that it is almost evening, and I can't believe what I am about to do next. I am Lucy Lamb, I think, and I am about to hop on my babysitter's motorcycle!

I learn a whole bunch of VERY important things next, which fit into a good news/bad news list:

1. Good news: I am very good at making Rick Hinkley laugh. He

calls me quirky, which I think is
a compliment.

2. Good news: I have a stunt
double. A stunt double is a
person who rides around
Montreal on a motorcycle,
pretending to be me, Lucy
Lamb, while I sit safely inside
a trailer.

3. Good news: This also means
that I DO NOT have to slide
down the mud mountain if I
don't want to! The stunt
double can do this.

4. Bad news: Emma laughed at me
   when I admitted that I thought
   I was going to have to slide
   down the mud mountain myself.
   She says movie stars never do
   their own stunts. Never.

5. Bad news: Emma Saxony is not a
   very good actress, so I am
   worried that Charlotte is at the
   wrong camp.

The reason I know this about Emma is
that it takes her about fifty takes to do every
scene. She doesn't seem to know her lines,
which is funny to me since now, after fifty

takes, even I know her lines. Also, she takes a lot of time to look at herself in the camera after each take. My mom and I have started rolling our eyes at each other, and then eventually crossing our eyes at each other,

while Emma fusses with her lipstick and squints at herself over and over again.

Then, just when I am feeling especially glad to be here, making a movie in Canada, just when the time comes for the stunt doubles (phew!) to hop on that motorcycle, something not so good happens as Emma and I stand clear and head back to our trailers. My fake babysitter says to me, "You know, you might be the reason I'm a little off right now. I think it's because this is your first movie. I can FEEL how NEW you are." She is enunciating perfectly. "Are you sure you want to be an actress and not, like, a comedian, or just a goofy kid who makes people laugh by falling all over herself? I mean, do you even know what KIND of actress you want to be? Think about it." She says this into the air and it just hangs over us like that horse-and-buggy smell.

I shrug. All because of mean Emma Saxony, I am back to being my old shrugging self. No Swish girl *cha-cha-cha*, no sassy sister Sylvie, no waffle-making super-secret-spy-girl Lucy Lamb. Just good old, scrambled-eggs-and-chocolate-milk, shrugging Jules Bloom.

"What's wrong, Jules?" my mom asks when I get inside the trailer.

"Nothing," I say. "Nothing is wrong. Everything is perfect. Can we go back to the hotel now?"

She and Colby look at each other, we gather our things, and I find myself walking very fast toward Teddy and Big Henry at the hotel, hoping they haven't had all the fun without me.

Before we go up to our room, I ask my mom for her phone. I want to send an e-mail.

Dear Elinor,

I forgive you for not writing me back yet. Maybe you are with Abby and showing her how not to be a tourist in London. I wish I were with you instead of here, since Emma Saxony is NOT the nicest person I have ever met and she thinks maybe I shouldn't be an actress. The only good news I can tell you is that I don't have to go down

that big mudslide at the end. I only have to swim in the
mud pool. Much better, I guess. I hope you are having
the summer of your dreams.

Love,

Jules

"Better?" my mom asks.

"Yep," I say. I am not better at all.

The good news for me is that Teddy
and Big Henry and Grandma Gilda are
playing Uno on the bed when I get to
my room.

"Whoa," Teddy says. "Nice clown face."

"It's movie makeup, Lichtenstein,"
George says.

"What was it like?" Big Henry asks. "Are

you a real spy now? Was Rick Hinkley a good guy or a bad guy?"

"What does Emma Saxony smell like?" Teddy asks.

I squint at him. Sometimes even I can't believe how weird he is.

"Later," I say. "I will tell you more later. Right now, I just want to play Uno."

I am so glad that everything is normal inside the hotel room. I don't even bother taking off my Lucy Lamb makeup. I just plop right down and they deal me in.

Later, we go out for dinner and sit outside at a place the concierge recommended, and we have French fries, which are called *frites*, and maple-syrup ice cream. And I

wish my dad were here so he could figure
out the recipes for these things since I wish
I could eat them every day of my life. And I
wish that they made everything all better,
but they don't.

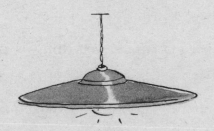

TAKE NINE

dads on airplanes, high-flying kids, and other northbound things

After two more days of filming in Montreal, we are on the road again. Mont-Tremblant, here we come! I can't wait because there was a brochure about this resort in the hotel lobby and there is going to be a luge slide and bungee-trampoline jumping in the village there, and even though I've been feeling pretty crummy ever since Emma Saxony made me feel like a clown, I'm thinking maybe a little bungee jumping would cheer me right up!

I take out my compass and stare at it. We are going north, toward my dad. That will cheer me up, too. My mom hands me her phone, open to an e-mail from strawberryscentedcharlotte.

Dear Jules,

Well, so I didn't get the main part in the play, but I play a very important part, which I think will definitely help me grow as an actress. I have to find something funny to think of because my character is someone who laughs a lot, which is kind of more your thing. How is Emma Saxony? Everyone here says Emma was just the greatest, most popular camper ever and that everyone knew she would be a star. Maybe you can tell her hi from Camp Lackahanna.

Love,

Charlotte

I am disappointed that the e-mail isn't from Elinor. What if her parents have decided to get back together and they are going to live happily ever after in London? I feel so bad that I don't want this to happen for Elinor. I mean, I DO want it to happen, but I'm worried that she'll never come back, and I'll be left with Stinkytown and third grade to deal with all on my own! I distract myself by writing back to my fruit-flavored former best friend.

Since Emma was kind of horrible to me and since I keep thinking about her asking me if I really wanted to be an actress and what kind and all that, and since she has made making this movie feel kind of awful instead of totally great, well, I want to write to Charlotte that Emma Saxony is a mean idol and not a teen idol. But something about Charlotte's e-mail sounds kind of sad, so I don't want to make anything worse for her.

Dear Charlotte,

I'm glad you are in a play and having fun, even if it isn't

the big starring role. I'm hoping I'll start having fun sometime VERY soon, since nobody told me that filming a movie isn't quite as much fun as you think. Also, I have to jump into a mud pile tomorrow, so maybe that will make you laugh for your play.

Love,

Jules

After yet another very long ride in the maxi-van, we arrive in a very pretty place with a big mountain and beautiful hotels and lots of people doing outdoor activities. We walk into the lobby dragging all of our pillows and things, and then I just drop it all. I see my dad! I run to him and he picks me up and I don't ever want to let go. But I have to let go when Big Henry yanks on my legs so hard, he almost pulls off my pants!

"You all are a sight for sore eyes!" my dad says. "Even the crazy lady!" Grandma Gilda jabs my dad in the side and then they hug. We all laugh, and the Lichtensteins go to their room and we go to ours, and Big Henry and I can't stop talking about everything that's happened so far. We have a whole afternoon as a regular family on

vacation before I have to become a movie actress again.

We are sitting at an outside café eating *frites* when my mom hands me yet another e-mail from Charlotte — I don't think they keep people very busy at her camp. I thought she was supposed to be white-water rafting and riding around in golf carts!

Dear Jules,

I think that will make me laugh for the play. It reminds me of your worm swimming pool. Remember when you told me you would save me some mud because it's good for my face? Well, there you go. It will be like a facial — at a spa! My so-called friends here don't even believe that you are the same Jules Bloom who is going to be in a movie with Emma Saxony, so do a good job. I can't wait till they see I was telling the truth.

Love,

Charlotte

I show the e-mail to my mom.

"I think Charlotte has been saying actual nice things about me," I say.

"Sounds like she was bragging about you," my mom says.

"I really thought she could only brag about herself," I say. "Maybe I should tell her about what a jerk Emma Saxony is because maybe that would make her feel better."

"Do you think that would make Charlotte

feel better, or would it make you feel better?" my mom asks.

"Is this like Daddy making me investigate things? That kind of a question?" I ask.

"I am just saying that maybe you could do something that would help Charlotte with her so-called camp friends," my mom says.

I get an idea right then and there.

We walk around the village, and then Big Henry and I spot the bungee-jumping thing. Kids are flying all around over there. Hank and I make a run for it.

My parents catch up to us and say, "Not right now, guys. You will get to go, just not right now."

"Why not?" I ask. "Tomorrow we start filming again and there won't be time."

"We talked about it with Colby," my dad says, "and we all think it's just the littlest bit risky, Jules. Once the movie is finished filming, you can bounce all you want."

I know if I act very mad and very frustrated that they will give me the lecture

about how I am making a choice to pursue acting, so I don't act mad. Well, I do, but not whiny mad. Just inside-mad.

We walk around a whole lot longer, and I am tired and bored and all I can do is watch other kids go on the bungee and the luge. And I'm sure Big Henry is pretty mad that all because of me, he can't go, either.

"Jules," my mom says to me back in the hotel lobby, "how are you?"

"I'm fine," I say. This is my plan. I'm fine. Fine, fine, fine.

"It doesn't seem like you're fine. It's been a long week already, and now you are about to shoot a whole bunch of scenes, and I know that Emma isn't exactly the sweetest, and now we've said no to the bungee, and

I'm wondering how you're keeping every-thing inside so neat and tidy?"

I start to feel shaky in my knees when she says all this, and I just wish she had left me alone. Now I feel like I'm going to explode in the French lobby with all the French-speaking children who I'm completely afraid to talk to since I never learned French the way I planned.

I walk out into the air and I start to cry. My mom follows me, and my dad and the others head up to the rooms.

"I guess I'm a little nervous, but only a LITTLE, and not like I usually am, and I just wanted for once not to be nervous and for everyone to think I could handle some-thing without tripping or throwing up or whatever!" My mom hugs me. "But now I just want to feel normal again. I want to hear English and I want to play with Elinor and maybe I even want to, I don't know, go to camp or something." I can't believe I say this, but it is true.

"That sounds like a lot of stuff to be keeping inside, and it's all fixable stuff," she says.

I believe her when she says this, but everything still feels a little bad, especially with all those kids bouncing high up in the air — having real fun, normal fun — right before my eyes.

The only good thing is that when we finally get back to the room, I have an e-mail from Elinor waiting for me.

Dear Jules,

I haven't wanted to write to you because my wonderful summer has turned not so wonderful. My parents are getting divorced. And on top of that, my dad wasn't even telling the truth when he said he would be here all the time for me. He's been working like crazy and my old friends are all at camp, so thank goodness Abby was here for two days and I got to show her around with my mom. And thank goodness I at least get to come back to New York City and to you and even Teddy and maybe a worm swimming pool.

Tell me something that will cheer me up. Is Emma Saxony still being horrible? She just needs Lucy Lamb to show her who's boss!

Love,

Elinor

I feel so bad that I wished for this. I can't even answer her right away. I feel bad that I've been mad at her, and that I got mad that my dad didn't come on the road trip with us, and that I got mad that I couldn't bungee jump. All while Elinor is having the worst summer ever.

I try to sleep because we have to be on set very early in the morning, but I stay awake for too long, thinking about Elinor and Charlotte and how I wish we were all at the school playground, instead of in three different parts of the world.

The next bunch of days come and go without me even seeing Big Henry or Teddy or even George. I am rehearsing lines, changing outfits, getting made up, trying not to fall asleep sitting there, watching Emma Saxony boss everyone around and watching Rick Hinkley be a real blockbuster hero. He's my new favorite movie star.

Finally, we wrap it up for the day and we have some free time, so Rick takes Colby and me on a hike to see the mudslide. As it turns out, Lucy Lamb gets Rick and Emma into all kinds of trouble, but she helps Rick figure out that Emma is the bad guy — the guy they are trying to stop. Emma Saxony is the villain, and even though it is Lucy's fault that Rick goes flying down a mudslide, it is the mudslide and Lucy Lamb that actually save the day, capturing Emma

Saxony in mud and stopping her in her tracks.

"You are one great actress, kid," Rick Hinkley says to me. Colby smiles at this and gives me a little push.

"Thanks," I say. "This is my first movie."

"Well, let's hope you stay you. I don't really see you turning into a fussy kind of actress anyway." I think he thinks Emma Saxony is fussy. "You are more of a hockey-player type actress, I think." I get the feeling that Rick Hinkley and I think alike. I love the idea that I am a hockey-player type actress. I picture myself with black goop under my eyes and a hockey mask, and I am facing off against Emma Saxony.

"Can't wait to slide down this baby," he says, looking at the mudslide.

"You don't have a stunt double?" I ask.

"Not for this. I think it'll be fun," he says.

"Do you think I could do it? Without a stunt double, I mean?" I ask.

"Sure! Kids do things like this all the time where I'm from," he says.

I squint my eyes and try to picture the hill in my neighborhood that leads down from Riverside Drive into Hippo Playground turning into a giant mudslide and all of the children of the Upper West Side sliding down it and into the park.

"Not where I'm from," I say.

"Rick!" Colby says now. "I don't know how Jules's parents will feel about this."

"Will Emma use her stunt double?" I ask.

"What do you think?" he asks. And then we all laugh.

TAKE TEN

small-time movie directors, muddy waters, and the fate of a certain rubber-duck hero

Dear Elinor,

You will not believe this, but I am going to do the mudslide

without a stunt double. Rick Hinkley is doing it himself,

too, and I saw the slide and thought it looked like fun,

and I told Colby I wanted to do it and then she talked to

the director and my parents and a lawyer and they all agreed that it isn't all that dangerous and that it would actually be a better scene if I do it — there will be close-ups of me going down instead of just shots of my body double, which is what Emma will have. I will do my own stunts because I am a hockey-player type actress. This is what Rick said.

I am very sad that your parents are getting divorced, and I hope I can be a good friend to you the way you always are to me. Picture me sliding through mud to cheer yourself up!

Love,

Jules

The last scene of the movie isn't filming until tomorrow afternoon because we need blazing-hot sun. So I get to stay up late after dinner and walk around the village and watch Teddy and Big Henry go on luge ride after luge ride while I cheer them on with my dad's video camera. This is my job since I can't actually *do* anything. I am the director.

"Let's go get in that bungee line," my dad says now. "All of us."

I stop walking and look at my parents. "I thought you said I couldn't do the bungee until after filming," I say.

"Well, that was before you became a stunt-person," he says.

"We're all gonna do it," my mom says.

"Even George?" I say.

"No way, José," she says. "I'm just here to laugh at your parents."

We run through the gate and we all get strapped into our bungees.

"I'm a little nervous," I say. I say this out loud for the first time all summer.

"Remember when we shouted our summer wishes onto Broadway?" my mom asks.

"Yep." That feels like a year ago, but it's only been a couple of weeks.

"Remember my positive affirmations?" Grandma Gilda shouts, as the rest of us get lifted up off the little trampolines.

I smile. This helped a lot with the sitcom. "Yep," I say.

"Remember the chocolate cake batter flinging all around the kitchen?" my

dad asks. I smile and look down at the mountain below me.

"Remember Bat Duck?" Big Henry asks. At this, I crack up.

"Yep."

The guy pushes me onto the trampoline with so much force I go flying, and I flip in the air and all those butterflies are going crazy. And then I see Big Henry out of the corner of my eye, his little body jumping up and down on the bungee cord.

"Do it for Bat Duck!" he shouts into the Canadian sky.

I look at him. *Okay*, I think. *I will.*

And the next day, I do.

I am running as fast as I can toward that mudslide when Rick's character says, "Lucy, jump!"

I take one look at that mud pit, pretend it is giant bowl of chocolate decaf cake batter, and I jump. I slide down with mud spraying all around me, and I am going fast, but it

isn't a rocky, bumpy ride, because they put plastic under the mud, which you don't see when you go to the movies, but it's there! I let out a big, fat, happy scream because it is the best feeling I have ever had, and then we all crash into the mud pool at the end and Rick stands up and says, "We got her!"

Then he puts Emma Saxony in handcuffs, and Emma and her character are

miserable and covered in mud. We all say a few more lines to each other, and then I hear, "Cut!"

I jump up and down in the mud and the director says the take was perfect, and he even lets Big Henry jump in the mud pool with us.

Then, the most amazing thing happens. Big Henry swims to me!

"You did it," he says.

"YOU did it," I say.

"I've been working on it with Daddy to surprise you," he says.

We all get out of the mud after a while, and I walk over to Emma, who is cleaning mud out of her ears. "Could I get your autograph?" I ask.

"Uh, sure," she says, kind of laughing. "I didn't know you were a fan."

"It's not for me. It is for my good friend Charlotte, who is at Camp Lackahanna, and she really loves you and her friends don't believe I'm in a movie with you, so could you write something nice so she can prove it?"

My mom takes my hand now, which is probably why Emma agrees. She gives Emma some paper and a pen.

Dear Charlotte,
    Your friend Jules is a real hoot. Give kisses to Camp Lackahanna for me!
    Xoxo,
    Emma Saxony

She signs her name in big teen-idol handwriting and hands me the paper.

"Thanks," I say. She turns away and then I think of something else I really want to say. "Emma!" She turns back to me. "About what you said in Montreal, I figured out what kind of actress I want to be — a hockey-player type actress," I say, and I smile a big Lucy Lamb physical-comedy smile.

Then Emma Saxony does something very Jules-like. She shrugs.

I made Emma Saxony shrug!

☆ ☆ ☆ ☆ ☆

After a few more days of real vacation, we say good-bye to the Lichtensteins and to

Canada. Teddy says he'll write from science camp, and I'm glad. I've gotten used to getting a lot of e-mail from my faraway friends.

We get all the way home to New York City a lot faster by airplane than by maxi-van. And when we get inside our lobby, Joe hands me a piece of turquoise mail. It's a birthday card from Elinor. She thought I would be here for it, I realize. And then he hands Big Henry a package — from Plattsburgh. "Bat Duck!" Hank says when he opens it. I am so relieved I start laughing hysterically.

"I can't wait to show everyone at camp how I can swim," my brother says.

"And I can't wait to be there to see it!" I say. We all decided on the plane that I would go to camp for a few weeks, too. My parents think it would help me feel like things were normal again, and I kind of agree.

And then Mom's phone rings. I think it is going to be Grandma Gilda making sure we got home all right and wanting to tell us about getting back to Florida just in time for a heat wave. But it isn't.

"It's Colby," my mom says to us. Then she picks it up and listens for a while.

"What is it?" I ask.

"You better enjoy 'normal' while it lasts," my mom says. "The sitcom was picked up. It's going to be a real show on TV — are you ready to be sassy Sylvie for a while?"

"Uh, YES!" I shout. Then I do a little Sylvie dance.

I'm ready for anything.

ACKNOWLEDGMENTS

On a road trip, I would first and foremost bring my brother, Michael Levine, who would make me spit out Easy Cheese and crackers with his backseat antics, and I would bring my mom, Gail Levine, who is even more entertaining on the road (and also a race car driver in disguise), and my dad, Charles Levine, who is a born explorer and also has mad map skills. I would always bring my adventurous and encouraging husband, Jon Ain, and our backseat drivers, Grace and Elijah. For laughs and support, I wouldn't mind putting my feet out the window with Rhonda Penn Seidman, Denise Goldman, Amy Flisser, Diana Berrent, Kim Lichtenstein, Denise Benun, Jill Grinberg, and Jenne Abramowitz, who would wear a cowboy hat — making our road trip feel all honky-tonk and, therefore, legit.

Many, many thanks also to the Dolphin Bookshop in Port Washington for providing me with so much support and a cozy place to write.

For a sneak peek at Jules's
next starring role, turn the page!

★ ★ ★

STARRING

Jules

(THIRD GRADE DEBUT)

"Ah! Bloom, Jules," my new teacher, Mr. Santorini, says, looking at a list he's holding in his hand. He walks over to me with his hand out. "Very nice to meet you." When I look at him closely, I realize he looks a little bit like Captain von Trapp in *The Sound of Music*, if Captain von Trapp would ever wear a Hawaiian shirt, that is. I'm just hoping he doesn't have a whistle.

I put my hand out and let him shake it. "Hmmm," he says. "Let's try that again. This time when I shake, shake back, sailor." I know what he means about the shake because this is how Colby Kingston, my agent, shakes hands. I just didn't know it was okay to shake a teacher's hand this way. I also don't know why he's calling me "sailor."

I grab on and shake firmly this time. I feel like my TV character, Sylvie, would handle all of this better than I am handling it, and I also think that this quirky Mr. Santorini would like Sylvie better than Bloom, Jules — worm-digging Upper West Sider.

BETH AIN was raised in Allentown, PA, but fell in love with New York City first as a little girl after hot pretzels from a corner stand warmed her up on a cold winter day, and again later, right after she knocked the mirror off of a city bus with her U-Haul the day she moved in. The driver quickly forgave her and she quickly decided it was the greatest city on earth. She did eventually head for the hills of Port Washington, Long Island, where small-town life has no shortage of inspiration, and where she can see the Empire State Building on her morning run — making it pretty easy to imagine what Jules is up to over there.

★ A STAR IS ★ BORN!

STARRING Jules (IN DRAMA-RAMA)
BETH AIN

STARRING Jules (AS HERSELF)
BETH AIN

STARRING Jules (SUPER-SECRET SPY GIRL)
BETH AIN

STARRING Jules (THIRD GRADE DEBUT)
BETH AIN

READ THEM ALL!

PRAISE FOR STARRING JULES (AS HERSELF):

★ "Vivacious Jules Bloom, with her singular wardrobe and all-around flair for the dramatic, hopes to accomplish a great deal before she turns eight . . . a truly funny narrative voice; her personality, misunderstandings, and tendency to overthink things are the driving force behind the story. . . . Fans of Judy Moody, Clementine, and other iconoclastic heroines will love getting to know Jules and look forward to the next book in this planned series."

—*Publishers Weekly* (starred review)